MONTREAL IN 15 CHAPTERS

It is my honour to be publishing short stories by Robert Markland Smith. He has been a literary figure on and off the margins of Montreal culture since the late 1960s. As he'd be the first to tell you, he has suffered with mental health challenges for decades, but he also continues to write, and support a family, including a wife and daughters. Like Job, he is a lucky man, if cursed. As this book will show, he is a gifted writer, with an immediately convincing voice. Moreover, his sense of compassion and humour flashes out, even while some of the tales portray the ludicrous, sometimes cruel, absurdities of being human. There are few if any writers working in English who better capture the Montreal sensibility – worldly but also, sometimes, down at heels, even lost. I happen to think that this 'outsider' writer has more than a bit of genius to him, and something of Dostoevsky, or maybe Bukowski, as well as other Beat writers. He deserves a wider international audience, and hopefully, with this funny, startling and original book, he will find one.

– Dr Todd Swift, Publisher

Robert Markland Smith

Montreal in 15 Chapters

First published in 2020
by Black Spring Press

Suite 333, 19–21 Crawford Street
Marylebone, London W1H 1PJ
United Kingdom

Typeset by Subash Raghu
Graphic design by Edwin Smet

ISBN 978-1-913606-26-8
www.eyewearpublishing.com

Dedicated to Bonnie, Isabelle, Cordelia and Shayne.

TABLE OF CONTENTS

THE MARQUIS DE SADE DOESN'T LIVE HERE ANYMORE

Do you remember being seventeen-years-old, and coming of age? Do you remember what prompted you to change from a jock to a joe college and from then, to become a bohemian? Somehow, the Church didn't speak to you any longer, your parents didn't seem very hip and the internal politics and dynamics of your family seemed morbid and repressive, didn't they? You argued about labour unions with your dad, and he kept telling you that you were imagining things, and he wondered what they were teaching you in college... You read *Les Fleurs du mal* by Baudelaire, you read the Comte de Lautréamont, and that figures, because you were a literature student. When you first started college, you tried to join a frat, but they rejected you because you wore a goatee and a tiki around your neck. You attended a couple of chug-a-lug parties, watched a couple of frat movies about becoming a successful businessman, and you weren't interested. You cultivated a taste for jazz, and long before you had peers, or friends your own age, you went to clubs like L'Ermitage, on Côte-des-Neiges, like the Black Bottom, on St. Antoine Street, and finally, the Penelope, on Stanley Street, in Montreal, of course.

You were acquiring a sense of identity that lasted through most of your adult life.

When you first moved to Montreal, your father set you up with his cousin Maurice's daughter. Now, Maurice would come to your house and argue that at every session of the United Nations, they should begin with the Lord's Prayer. In other words, he was a bigot. And even when you were sixteen-years-old, you knew that at the UN there were Muslim countries, and communist countries, and you were kind of embarrassed by your father's cousin. As for the daughter, well, you remember taking her to a Jacques Lussier concert at Place des Arts, and she commented that she only liked the Bach, whereas you liked the jazz, and you remember walking her home to Outremont, across Park Avenue, and she said, with scorn in her voice, that these immigrants were so vile and stupid and dirty and disgusting. In other words, she was a tight-assed little bitch, and her pastime was to sit by candlelight in her bedroom and listen to Bach and read Kierkegaard. Mind you, there is nothing wrong with Bach or Kierkegaard, but when you are sixteen, you are expected to have a bit more piss-and-vinegar than that. You would take her out on dates, and sit in the park, in Outremont, and she looked so prissy and uptight that you never even made a pass at her. (I guess you secretly hated her.)

So, to sum up, you were dissatisfied with the father's cousins. You wanted to hoist anchor and leave traditional ways behind.

One night, and it was perhaps in February of 1966, you were sitting in the Bistro on Mountain Street by yourself, having a beer, because that's what macho guys did, they drank hard. (Perhaps you were also a budding drunk, but that's another story.) Anyway, you were sitting there, by the door, when in walked a college buddy, Gabriel. He was in your English Romantic poetry class at Loyola College, and he joined you for a beer, and you two got to talking, and he asked you if you wanted to go to a really neat place nearby.

So, you finish your beer, and you both walk down to a place called The Hawaiian Lounge, on Stanley Street, right beside the Esquire Show Bar. You walk in, and you've been there perhaps ten minutes, when you start noticing something funny, something strange going on. For instance, there is a lady with a platinum-blonde wig and a beauty spot on her face, and wearing a fancy white blouse with frills and a crotch-high mini skirt, and she comes up to you with a dirty smile and pinches your cheek. And when she speaks to you, she has a man's voice, a deep, sexy, raspy voice, and she tells you her name is Sugar. And there is something going on here, and you don't know what it is, do you, Mister Jones?

And you look around the room, and it's full of boys dressed up as girls and girls dressed up as boys, and you are a middle-class Catholic kid, and you decide to play it by ear. You sit with Gabriel and order a beer, and you watch the floorshow, because there is a huge stage right plop in the middle of the bar. You watch nervously, while a stripper dressed at first as a woman, strips down to a pair of underwear, and oh my god! it's a man, and he starts cracking a whip, and jeez, this is vulgar. You watch a lesbian singer called Carole Berval belt out Otis Redding songs about girlfriends. And there is Alice.

At the next table over, there is a cute young thing with long, curly black hair, and the blackest, darkest, most evil mascara you have ever seen, and she is wearing a micro mini skirt, and she is sitting with a butch that looks like E.G. Robinson, with short black hair greased back, and wearing a man's suit, and smoking a cigar. Anyhow, the girl is called Alice, and she is dancing on stage, and you ask her to dance, and she dances with you, and you speak French together, and you are a bit disappointed that she is so vulgar. Now, your sun is in Virgo, your moon is in Scorpio and your rising sign is in Scorpio, which means you are in love with Alice, the woman in black. Anyway, after a while, Gabriel tells you not to dance with her anymore, because her butch lover wants to kill you.

And Gabriel keeps going to the other side of the room, and disappearing for half an hour at a time, he goes to the other side of the stage, and meanwhile, someone from over there keeps buying you beer. You ask the waiter who is ordering you free beer, and he says it's someone over there. So what the hell, you don't care, you drink the beer first and figure you'll ask questions later. After all, a free beer is a beer, right?

So this goes on until about one o'clock in the morning, when Gabriel tells you he's leaving. And you tell him you're staying behind, and you're going to watch the show by yourself. And the band keeps playing, and you are trying to look hip, and finally, it's three o'clock in the morning, and it's closing time. Last call.

At this point, a big, muscular guy built like a professional boxer comes to your table, and he's wearing a suit, and he says to you, "Come with me." You ask what is going on, and he says your friend sold you to him for fifteen dollars, and you now have to go with him. That goddamn Gabriel. So that's who was buying you free beer from across the stage! So what do you do?

Okay, let's go. You get your winter coat, and you (slowly walk down the stairs with the boxer, and you (slowly open the door, and you (slowly and carefully walk down to the street, and THEN, BY GOD! YOU HEAD FOR THE HILLS, RUNNING AWAY FROM TROUBLE, AND YOU TURN AND YELL AT THE GUY, IN FRENCH, "I'M SORRY, I AM NOT A HOMOSEXUAL!" And he doesn't run after you, he just stands there, brokenhearted as his date runs away.

Well, you kept going back to the Hawaiian Lounge, for about six weeks, and buying drinks for Alice, and you phoned the cousin's daughter, and you told her you were leaving her for a lesbian from downtown, and she was shocked. But then Gabriel had the kindness to tell you that Alice was NOT in love with you, she was REALLY a prostitute and she was ONLY interested in you because she thought you had money. So what goes around comes around, and you were disappointed, to say the least. You were still a naïve bourgeois kid, and it took some time before you woke up, quite a long time indeed.

THE MAN WHO HATED LEONARD

Everyone loves Leonard. But as for me, I used to hate Leonard Cohen. I would go to parties, and this poet would be boasting of having had breakfast with Leonard, and having shown Leonard his manuscript. And yes, Leonard loved his manuscript, and do you know Leonard? Why yes, I know Leonard. I was asked to write an epitaph for him when he dies. And yes, everyone I know in Montreal – and his dog – knew Leonard.

Except for me. I didn't know Leonard. I would see his books sold in the late seventies in used bookstores. And every time I turned the TV on, there was Leonard. OOOOOH, how I used to cringe whenever I saw Leonard on TV. And as for his ex-girlfriend Suzanne, well she cut me off because she thought I was crazy and dangerous. But I am not dangerous. I just told Suzanne that my parents used to hypnotize me into being a spy for them among the artist crowd. I told her that because I was off my medication, and well, I had to tell her something…

But I am not dangerous. I just hate Leonard.

Let me explain why. I used to write poetry. Well, probably pretty bad poetry. I guess it was bad, because every publisher in sight and every magazine editor in Canada rejected my material. I even contemplated making it in the States to be accepted here. So I tried even harder to get published. Something was missing. I was not Leonard Cohen. So I hated him.

Nothing personal, Mr. Cohen. But you could blow your nose on a piece of paper, submit it to McClelland & Stewart, and they would sell it. Worldwide.

I used to wonder if Leonard had sold his soul in order to make it. I never found out.

I saw Leonard live twice. The first time was in December 1969, the year the police went on strike in Montreal. I ended up in the Douglas that year. And didn't Leonard come and give a concert for the mentally ill that winter, at the Dalse Center. I was there in the audience, and I was thrilled. Hey, it was a good concert. I had had a bad trip on acid, and Leonard said to the patients, "You people are the political prisoners of our society." Just what I wanted to hear, because I was a politico. A radical. I wanted to plant bombs, but didn't know how.

Anyway, that was in 1969. In 1983, I was out of the Douglas, one day in October. I had just gotten out, by the way, when I was in a smoked meat restaurant on the Main called – what else? The Main, when suddenly, I saw him. Him. You know. The ladies' man. He was dining with two beautiful ladies at the table next to mine. I whispered to the waitress, "Excuse me, is that Leonard Cohen?"

"Uh-hm," she whispered, meaning yes.

So I surreptitiously finished my smoked meat sandwich, and got my nerve up. I walked right up to the next table over and asked him, boldly I must say, "Are you Leonard Cohen?"

And he looked at me right in the eye, without batting an eyelash, and exclaimed, in a disarming way:

"YES I AM!!!" And I immediately began to stutter, "M-m-m-my na-na-name is Ro-ro-ro-robert S-s-s-smith…"

I started fidgeting as I stood in front of their table, and I said, stuttering some more, "I-I-I-I ma-ma-mailed you my boo-boo-book I've be-be-been so happy since I go-go-go-got my lobotomy."

I managed to blurt that out, and he almost smiled as he answered me, "Yes, it is sitting on my coffee table at home. Tell me, did you really have a lobotomy!!?"

And I burst out with, "No-no-no, but I just got out of the Douglas!!" I said it so fast I wasn't even sure they heard me. Then I added, "I go-go-got your address from my fr-fr-friend Jo-jo-John Max…"

And once again, he gave me a disarming Zen master smile, as I turned around abruptly and walked embarrassed out of the restaurant. As I was walking out, one of the ladies dining with Leonard whispered to him, "That man was just like a little mouse!"

And I went home and proceeded to have a nervous breakdown which lasted ten months.

SOMEDAY MY PRINCE WILL COME

I had been in Douglas Psychiatric Center for several weeks, and it was during the October crisis in 1970. My friend Alex Duarte had gotten a day pass to take me out for a walk. It was a few weeks after the actual crisis and Alex took me out that morning to see all the Canadian soldiers occupying the city. The sky was gray, there was a cold breeze, and no one on the streets. We went near Montreal city hall, and there were troops stationed with machine guns all around the building. They were in uniform, wearing battlegear but there was no battle. It was what the Prime Minister, Pierre Trudeau called an "apprehended insurrection," and the province of Quebec was under arrest, under the War Measures Act. At every government building, there were soldiers standing erect, at attention.

It was a Sunday morning, and behind city hall, near the metro station, we were walking around thinking over what had transpired. I was all screwed up on largactyl, on a massive dose of neuroleptic medication, when we bumped into a few comrades of mine from the *Front de libération du Québec,* girls and guys, maybe four or five of them, whom I had met that autumn while going to demonstrations and riots and attending cell meetings. They were perhaps twenty-years-old. I was twenty-one, and when they saw how frozen I looked from the shoulders on up, one of the ladies said to me, "Y t'ont pas manqué, hein?" which would translate as "They really nailed you to a cross, eh?" I was telling them that I was a patient in the College and was out on a day pass. I could barely talk. Society was brainwashing me. If the doctors couldn't give me a lobotomy, they reached the same effect of total compliance by injecting me with massive doses of medication. There was no apprehended insurrection in sight, only soldiers paranoid as hell and expecting a jack-in-the-box to spring out of the sidewalks.

I looked up and saw the oppressive skyline of downtown Montreal against a sky as gray as a machine gun or a prison wall.

All civil rights were cut off for five months and people were getting arrested and interrogated for no reason. Alex's friend Barry is a painter and he had a book on cubism in his apartment, so when the soldiers raided his apartment, they thought the book was about Cuba. Anyone left of center was denounced, arrested and checked. I know a waitress who had a black boyfriend and she was arrested for suspicion.

Democracy used a fascist law, a wartime law, to protect itself and enforce conformity. There were no more bombs, no more demonstrations, no more windows smashed. This was law and order.

I looked up at the sky and a few seagulls landed beside us, squawking, demanding food, protesting.

THE LANGUAGE POLICE

B eing a French Canadian, I had never understood the concerns of English-speaking Quebecers regarding Bill 101 and the language laws. My father had been a member of the Société Saint-Jean Baptiste and l'Ordre de Jacques Cartier. My mother's sister and father, that is my aunt and my grandfather, had been involved in l'Action catholique years ago. I had been taught, like most French Canadians, that "les Anglais" were all rich, unemotional, frigid lovers, hostile to us, prejudiced against French Canadians, arrogant and smug. Their only goal in life was to assimilate French Canadians. What is worse, some of them were *Protestants*!

However, I started getting an insight into the Anglo concerns and acquiring sympathy for Quebec Anglophones, in 1989, when I was working as a French-English translator for the Ministry of Education under Claude Ryan. Everyone in the office was an Anglophone but me, and the boss couldn't even speak French. So we had nothing to do with applying language laws.

What my job did involve was translating Quebec academic programs into English, and once in a while, into French. One afternoon, I was in the middle of translating a technical manual about the chemicals used in making paints, and I couldn't find some terms. I looked and looked in computers, data banks and dictionaries, but could find nowhere the names of these chemicals in French. So, being a good translator, I used the phone book. I thought I would call a paint company or a paint dealer and ask for my French equivalents over the phone.

I found a small paint dealer on Cavendish Boulevard, in NDG. I dialed their main number.

"Hello, could I speak to your translator, please?"

"Who's calling, may I ask?"

"My name is Robert Smith, and I am calling from the Quebec government. Could I speak to your company translator, please?"

(Aside, to another employee) "It's the government. They want to know if we have a translator!"

(Answering me, a moment later) "I am afraid we don't have a translator. Can I help you?"

"Well, I wanted to know if your sales catalogue is translated into French..."

(Aside, to the other employee) "George, do something. It's the language police! We're in trouble! Do something, quick!"

(Answering me, a moment later) "Does this have anything to do with Bill 101?"

"No, no, no. I am a translator, and I am calling from the Ministry of Education. I just want to find some French terms."

"You mean to say, you're calling from the Quebec government and you don't know French? Or you want to check up on us to know if we speak French?"

"No, I just want to know if you could give me some terms from your sales catalogue."

"You want to check the quality of our French?"

"No, I simply want to find some terms in French."

(Aside, to another employee) "George, what do I tell him?"

(Answering me, a moment later "I am afraid our sales catalogue is in English only, but I promise you we'll have it translated soon."

"No problem."

"Does that mean you're going to send the inspectors here? Our signs in front of the store are bilingual."

"Look, I am just a translator."

"But you're a *fonctionnaire*."

"Yes, but... Thanks anyway. No hard feelings."

"Bye."

I finally did find my French expressions from a federal phone-in data bank. A terminologist was glad to oblige. As for the employees of the small paint dealer on Cavendish, either they have moved to Ontario by now or they are still waiting for the inspectors to show up with a warrant for their arrest.

THE GLITTERING PLEASURE DOME

"For all nations have drunk of the wine of the wrath of her fornication, and the kings of the earth have committed fornication with her, and the merchants of the earth are waxed rich through the abundance of her delicacies."

(Revelations 18:3)

The barker cries out, for all to hear along the street, "Step right up, folks! Come and see the wonders of the world! We have got women who strip down and turn you into animals, like Circe of old! We have got freaks who can recite poetry inspired by the devils and evil spirits of Babylon! Step right up, men, women, children, it's the greatest show on earth!"

And the lights behind him are flashing, strobe lights roam up and down the strip, and there are wild jazz saxophones screeching. The young children walk up to the barker, and stare at him in bewilderment.

He continues, "We've got Barbie dolls for you kids, and depraved Disney videos with happy endings for all of you! You, son, come up front here." And one little boy with stars in his eyes approaches the snake oil salesman.

"Yes, sir," he whispers, his tongue hanging out of his rosy lips.

"Son, tell me," the barker howls into his microphone. "Do you like war? Do you like blood and guts and gore?"

"Yessir," the little boy's eyes light up with an evil glare.

"Well, we have got computer games in which real soldiers shoot real bullets at real peasants, and it is all yours for a few pennies a minute. So step right in, son!"

And the little boy walks in, enticed. He enters the giant arcade, with the sirens whistling, and the lewd pictures of women in bikinis, and his mother cries after the little boy, but he is lost in a maze of demonic children.

There is now a crowd of spectators approaching. The barker is on fire from hell, and he is yelling now: "Who wants a sports car that shoots bullets like James Bond's vehicle? Who wants a Batmobile that can fly through a building as impregnable as the World Trade Center? You sir, you look like you are eager to kick ass!"

And another young man pays his ticket to the doorman, and disappears from the street into the glittering front door of the night club. His girlfriend is in shock, to lose her lover to such cheap attractions and cheap thrills.

Now the barker carries on, and he does a little dance around his white cane. He is wearing a glowing green bow tie, and waving around a top hat with the American flag on it. He spots a young girl out of the crowd. He grabs her attention and she is mesmerized. "You, there! Would you like men to worship the ground you walk on? Would you like to be as famous and sexy as Madonna?"

Her eyes light up and a smile stretches across her face, like a snake wrapping itself around her head. The barker continues: "Well, we have just the fashions for you! We have see-through blouses and skin-tight pants! Plus we have spiked heels that will make you look like a tramp! Hey, don't pass up this opportunity, step right up and pay the doorman. Ladies' night will be tomorrow night, so pay right up!"

And the teenage girl just can't resist, because they haven't taught her that in her school. She flows into the arcade, hissing like a boa constrictor. We never see her again.

"Finally, ladies and gentlemen, who wants to get rich quickly? Hey, we have internet sales in the billions of dollars, we have bogus prospectuses, insider trading, and you can even become politicians! You sir, wouldn't you like to sway the masses with your winning smile? Would you like to be a show-business star and run the government? Step right up!!" And one more young lawyer disappears into the babylonian arcade, never to reappear until he is recycled into one of the devil's disciples.

However, there is a homeless person in the crowd, a penniless hobo who wanders up and asks the barker, "What about me? Can I get in there? I haven't got the money to pay admission, but you can have my soul, buddy!"

But the crowd has now dissolved, and the doors to the night club are closing. The barker gives the homeless man a look of disdain and scorn, and states, for all to hear: "No, sir, here we only take cash or credit cards. We are not interested in your two-bit soul. Besides, the door is closing. We are not taking any more pleasure seekers tonight. Go to the Salvation Army, buddy, go to the mission and try to get a bed for the night. We are not a charity organization here. Besides, old man, the last shall be first and the first shall be last, haha."

The door closes. The barker has gone indoors. Suddenly, we can't hear the music; the flashing lights have abated. It is dark and silent on the main street. It can be Sainte-Catherine Street in Montreal, it can be somewhere in Soho, in London; it can be in Greenwich Village, in New York.

The lights are out, and the homeless person walks away, wondering what he is missing. He stumbles, because he has a bad leg. He searches through a garbage can, looking for a sandwich, and then finds a lit cigarette butt on the sidewalk. He glances back at the magic-theater night club, and then continues on his way, limping into the night.

The shadows swallow him up and cover him like a protective mantle. He disappears into an alley and we can't see him anymore.

Fade.

THE SATELLITE PROGRAM

From: Captain Klutz
To: Colonel Putz
Sent: Thursday, December 04, 2003 8:45 AM
Subject: Tracking homeless people

Dear Colonel,

As per our recent telephone conversation, I will soon forward you the reports concerning tracking homeless people. Our satellite program seems to be functioning adequately. And the homeless people are not aware that we are monitoring them, except for one Robert M. Smith.

You asked me recently for a breakdown and explanation of this tracking program. Here it is, as follows:

Our computers at the headquarters of the Royal Canadian Mounted Police are linked to American satellites in the atmosphere. The information obtained by the satellites through remote cameras is transmitted to our computers. The images are then deciphered and interpreted by means of sophisticated programs. The satellites follow homeless people around town. Their cameras take films and photographs of these homeless people, as the latter wander around aimlessly from shelters to soup kitchens to parks to alleys, etc.

The behavior patterns of the homeless people are then submitted to our analysts, who use advanced fractals mathematics to find patterns and therefore predict where the subjects will end up. Since there are 30,000 homeless people in Montreal alone, there are a plethora of films and photographs to store and interpret. The purpose of the tracking process is to enforce our control on the subjects. The rest of the city is predictable, but homeless people seem to wander aimlessly. And yet, our analysts claim that by following these derelicts around by remote cameras, they will lead us to Bin Laden and the whole Al Q'aida network in Montreal.

There is only one snag in our program.

One of these homeless persons, one Robert M. Smith, has somehow become aware that we follow him around, and is trying to fool us by deliberately wandering round in irrational patterns. The other derelicts only wander spontaneously from place to place, but Robert Smith seems to be using a ploy to destroy our computer programs. He can wander up and down the same street fifty times in a row, back and forth, and then suddenly veer off once we detect his behavior pattern.

Our satellites are also connected to television sets in bars and restaurants, which look at the customers. The images that customers see on television are only a facade. The real purpose of television is to watch the viewers. But once again, Robert M. Smith has done nasty things like turning the characters on television green on purpose and laughing insanely as news anchormen choke and gag.

Therefore, our hit men from the mafia are following this Robert M. Smith around and waiting for the perfect opportunity to assassinate him in cold blood. He seems to be aware that we are doing this, and has tried to sabotage our plans by walking around in irrational patterns that our computers cannot detect.

As for the general population, they would never believe that we partake in this level of sophistication. If the media blew the whistle and told them about our plans, the people would think we are joking with them. As usual, the totalitarian states are always elsewhere. The enemy is always Castro, Ho Chi Minh, Saddam Hussein, some totally demonized dictator Out There, but the people place their total trust in their leaders.

This type of psychological projection maintains the notion that everyone in Canada is innocent and harmless.

For further information, do not hesitate to contact me as usual.

Yours in Him,
Captain Klutz
RCMP
Surveillance Unit
Ottawa, Canada

STREET BUSINESS INC.

" **A** AAAGH!!" I woke up screaming, once again. My arms were flailing, caught in the bed sheets and I was in a cold sweat. I was trying to break out of a web, a spell, something demonic that recurred every night.

"Robert, are you all right?" That is my mother. She was just out in the hall, outside my room, gathering dirty clothes to prepare a load of laundry. She is fifty-something, and a single mom. She is doing her best, but she looks haggard this morning.

"I'm all right, mom, it's just that dream again!" She looks at me for a second, nods and goes about her business doing housework.

The dream went like this. I am inside the basement of a castle, and I am trying to find my way out. I go up staircases, as though going up into the steeple of a church, and down empty halls. Finally, while my enemies are in pursuit, I find a little door. It is really small. And I slip through this door, and suddenly, I am sliding, sliding down endless tunnels, like on a slide in the park, and it is dark, and no one knows about this exit except for me. The speed of the dream accelerates, as I run down downwards tunnels, and finally exit through a hole in the wall, and come out on the outside of a mountain on which the castle rests.

It is nighttime. I am now outdoors, and the mountainside is breathing, and lava like sweat is pouring down

25

the sides of the hill. I am then walking down a country road, where I cross clowns and freaks and snake oil salesmen walking the other way, and towards the end of the country road, there are herds of filthy pigs held in red pigpens. And it seems like that is the future of mankind, to turn into swine held in someone's animal farm. And then I wake up, sweating and oftentimes screaming for my life, until I realize I am awake.

Oh, let me introduce myself. I am Robert Markland Smith. I am sixteen-years-old, and the lady I just described earlier was my mother. My father was an alcoholic and just couldn't stand the pressures of family life. After something happened, he disappeared, and we rarely ever hear from him anymore. I am presently a student at Concordia University in Montreal, and my mother rents a house from her parents. She works part-time at the university or somewhere.

Now it is time for breakfast. Then I will have to pack my school bag and take off for school.

My mother looks tired. It is only 9:00 o'clock in the morning, and she already appears burned out. "You look tired, mom. Can't you get some rest?"

"It is just that I have been up since 5:30 this morning. I just wanted to finish the laundry before going to work." She is pausing to have a cup of coffee with me while I wolf down breakfast. "Robert, can't you eat a bit slower?"

She is a bit concerned because I am overweight. I am downright chubby, and the only reason that bothers me is that every now and then, some kid at university calls me "Fatso" or "Le gros Bob." I am mainly worried about my pimples. That is probably why I don't have a girlfriend. Or a boyfriend, because lately I don't know which way I swing. There is that boy in my French lab who looks so cute!

"Robert, why are you daydreaming? You have a class at 10:00."

"Sorry, mom." And off I go, without making my bed or picking up after myself. My room looks like the World Trade Center after September 11, a total mess.

Now I am on the bus, on the way to school. It is only a few blocks. I am spaced out this morning. That recurring dream about the mountain again. It shakes me up.

I am looking at people's ears and then their noses on the bus. Mainly business people on the bus this morning. All grown-ups. They look so solid, so monolithic, and I feel transparent and neurotic. They are even smug, I would say. I don't know, maybe it is the neighbourhood. Maybe these people have never stopped to think things over. That man sitting beside me looks like he is made out of stone. No ruffles, no wrinkles. He is reading the morning newspaper, like most people on the bus. And you know that the paper tells the truth!

Now I am at school. Philosophy class. English class. Go to the library. I saw a gorgeous girl at the library. She had a huge chest. I blushed when she smiled at me. Christ, I wish I wasn't a virgin! Girls can probably tell. She looked like a Playboy bunny. I wish I had the nerve to ask her for her phone number. All these inaccessible ladies! They must see right through me! Now I am dropping my library books all over the floor. The library security guard is giving me a dirty look. "Sorry, sorry!"

Anyway, I have to go to the downtown campus today. I am on the shuttle bus, with other students. Some guys are fooling around, others are talking to girls, but I am reading a textbook.

I noticed something today. I was just getting off the shuttle bus, which goes from one campus in suburbia to the downtown campus, when I saw a homeless person. And this person was eating out of a garbage can. I have seen homeless people before, I have read advertisements from charity organizations about the homeless, but I paused when I saw this man and I spaced out for several minutes. It was cold, because it is November going on December, and this man with a growth of beard and a scarf around his neck stared back at me. Then he waved his arm at me, as if to say hello, or was he beckoning me to come towards him – or to come into his world? He smiled at me, as though he recognized me! Who was he? Was it my father? I doubt it. But the homeless man, who was carrying bags full of newspapers in one hand, stood there smiling at me for a full minute. He was standing on the other side of the street. He was on Guy and de Maisonneuve Boulevard, and I was on the north side of the street. Then a bus rushed down the street between us, and when the bus passed, the man with the growth of beard had vanished. Was it an apparition? An apparition of my late father?

Come on, Robert. Come to your senses. I shook my head and rubbed my eyes. Pedestrians were racing past me, and cars were speeding down the boulevard. Then there was a trickle of snow, one or two snowflakes. Then it started to snow gradually more and more. I shivered, and remembered I had to go to the Hall Building to see someone.

I never mentioned that incident to my mother. When I came home, my mother had come back from work, and she was just preparing supper. "Did you have a good day?"

"Yes, but I saw a man – "

"And? What about him?"

"Oh, nothing. I have to read a chapter from my history book before supper. I only have three pages left in the chapter."

"How many pork chops?" My mother looked at me, inquiring.

"Oh, two is good." And I went off to my room to finish reading the book. I thought for a split second about the homeless man who had waved at me, but I dismissed it immediately. I could remember the look in his eye, a look of wisdom.

That was my first contact with *Them*.

★★★

In the next couple of days, I got a few more signs, omens, whatever you want to call them. This is totally absurd to me, by the way, but I couldn't help but notice.

For instance, yesterday, I was at the Loyola Campus of the university, after a class, and I was using the washroom. Right over the urinal, there was a graffiti that caught my eye: "Break on through to the other side." I had once heard that lyric in a song by Jim Morrison, of *The Doors*. That was a psychedelic band in the sixties, and I am a big fan of sixties music. I have a ollection of vinyl that includes four or five hundred records. And I have an old stereo record player that still works perfectly. But that lyric rang a bell, it made me space out for a minute, the same way the homeless guy did a few days ago. What is this other side? What does that song mean? Break on through to the other side! Very strange.

Nevertheless, I dismissed that sign also. Now I have been reading Jack Kerouac's *On the Road*, for an English class. Actually, the teacher recommended I read it, because I told him I am interested in the 1950s and 60s. And I wondered where and how I could find that level of adventure. And I was on the bus coming home from school, and it blew my mind, but two other people on the bus were reading the same book! There were three of us on the bus reading the classic by Kerouac. Now that was uncanny!

Tonight, I told my mother I felt like I was about to go through adolescence and I warned her I might do some strange or silly things. She seemed to handle it. She already knew this, she told me. She just told me not to drink like my father.

Later on that evening, I didn't share this with my mother, but an image flashed through my mind: I knew I was like a ship that was about to hoist anchor and sail off, away from traditional ways. I was about to wander off. I felt stifled living with my mother, but I couldn't tell her that. I wrote a note to myself to this effect, but I threw it in the garbage, lest mom see it and read it. I wouldn't want to upset her. And then I looked outside the window, and saw the moon looking mysterious out there in the sky, and I took a deep breath. I knew I wanted to experience life, to experience more than college life and living in a room with my mom. It was like a calling, a vocation. I felt led to go out and see life, see the world. And that world out there, that world beyond seemed full of promise. There were lots of beautiful women out there, lands to visit, books to read, smells, mountains, depths of the sea, and adventures.

"Robert, are you doing your homework?" It was my mom calling me back to reality. She was just standing outside the door to my bedroom, and she could sense I was thinking dangerous thoughts!

Reality just seemed to me so mundane, like bank accounts, walking down the same streets all the time, parking meters, the newspapers, the same old wars and strikes, the politicians, the college profs, the cafeteria at school, and church, when I used to be young. It was despicable. The routine, the boredom. Planning for your retirement. when you haven't lived. And keeping the same lousy job for thirty long years. I knew some Commerce students who had their whole career planned, from start to finish.

And I knew that somewhere out there, there was life, real life, strange lands, like Thailand or South Africa. Life in Canada was so colonial! People were dying before even being born.

Finally, I saw one more sign, one more invitation, one more calling, before it all happened. My friend Mary Wells invited me to go up to the mountain, on top of Mount Royal. And it was cold and windy. We went up by the Cote-des-Neiges Road side of the hill, and walked up the rickety stairs near the Boulevard. Once we hit the top of the mountain, we walked to the chalet. It was a Saturday, and I postponed doing homework for a day. At the chalet, we saw the strange homeless woman who haunts the building.

The chalet is a little restaurant set by a lake on top of Mount Royal, right in the middle of Montreal. And the homeless woman, who talks to herself, who has hair like the Medusa, who dresses in rags, who scurries about mumbling curses, stopped and looked at me. It was as if she knew me from somewhere. My friend Mary Wells asked me afterwards if I knew that woman. But I was in a world of dreams by now. I was awestruck by seeing the homeless woman. I didn't answer Mary. She asked me again, "Robert, who was that? Do you know her? Speak to me." But I kept looking back at the chalet as we walked away. I was mesmerized. The homeless woman was standing by the door of the restaurant, staring at me as I walked away. And she was saying something to me, but I couldn't make it out from so far away. I was now a hundred feet away.

Who were all these people that wandered the streets? Why did they seem to recognize me? And who am I that they should notice me? What is so special about me?

Mind you, I tried to dismiss those thoughts and concentrate on my everyday life. For a couple of weeks, I remembered the vagrants but then other things happened, and I got distracted. Until I broke on through to the other side.

★★★

Normally, I don't ever get drunk or take substances, because I don't want to end up like my dad. He used to scream and get violent when he drank. If the drink was his pacifier, it also agitated him. Especially when he was still thirsty and my mother wouldn't let him drink anymore. Then he got really rowdy. So I avoid alcohol and drugs.

Yet, tonight, I am sitting in a bar on Mackay Street, in Upstairs, and I am getting hammered. I am listening to some John Coltrane music on the PA system. And I feel blue.

But I catch myself. I am not going to end up like my father. I am still lucid enough to pay my tab and walk — well, stagger out of the bar. There are only a couple of other people in there, and no one notices me. No one notices me. I see an old wino across the street, peeing in the alley, and I just ignore him.

I walk to the Guy metro station, which is a block away. I take out my wallet, and find a bus ticket. I put my wallet back into my pants. I take the escalator down to the turnstiles. I pay my way and go into the metro station. I go down the escalator once again down to the platform. There is no one in the metro station but me. It is awfully dreadfully quiet. I start walking down the platform. There is no sound or rumbling of a metro within hearing distance. I am walking down the platform. Suddenly, I notice a small opening in the wall, a tiny aperture, a door with a light shining through it. I bend down, because I am curious. And now I feel led by the spirit to crouch down and crawl through the door. This door is about three feet tall and about two feet wide. Honest to god, I don't know why I am doing this. And I come through the door. I am on the other side of the door, and my feet slip. I am suddenly sliding, sliding, down a tunnel, and it is exhilarating, partly because I am drunk, partly because the slide downwards seems greased. I am zigzagging down the tunnel — where am I going? Now I do a somersault and land on my feet, and I am running down a tunnel that seems to lead to the center of the earth, and I can hear people running after me, or thundering hooves, and I am running, running, and losing my balance. Finally, I bump my head and knock myself out for a second. I end up in a pile of rubbish, and alone. There are rats scurrying about somewhere, I can hear their squeaky voices. They are gnawing at the stone wall surrounding me. I come to my senses, and rather than ask questions, I start climbing the stone wall, about ten feet up, and now I see a light at the end of the tunnel. I come out of a hole and out into the street.

But where am I? Is this Montreal? I don't feel the effect of the alcohol anymore. I am rather totally awake, painfully awake. There is a blinding light shining through everything even though a minute ago, it was nighttime. I look at my watch, and it is stopped. It seemed to have stopped at the time when I entered the metro station.

I am on a street — or what seems to be a street. It feels like high noon, but there are trees on this street, along the sidewalks, and the trees look spidery, alive and creepy. They have no leaves, and there is a wind blowing through the branches, and the branches are dancing a strange ballet. No there is no wind; it is the trees that are dancing. Otherwise everything is still. There are stores along the sidewalks, and the windows are all boarded up. The names of the stores are in a foreign language and a foreign alphabet. It is neither Chinese nor Persian. And there is no one on this street. I am here all alone, and all dirty from falling through that pit. There is soot on my clothes, and I seem to have ripped a hole in both my shoes. My toes are showing through the tip of the shoes.

For a split second, I think of my mother. What will I tell my mother? But suddenly, I see a Coke bottle fall from the sky and land in front of me, as though someone had thrown it at me. I look up and a bunch of wicked children are laughing and they throw another bottle at me. What is going on here? I am going to have to find shelter.

I see some strange gentlemen walking towards me. One of them is wearing a huge suit and has a parrot on his right shoulder. They approach, see my predicament and laugh at me. Right in my face. Why? What have I done to them? They both look intoxicated, and they wander off past me along the street and I can still hear them laughing. Then a blinding light hides them from my sight.

I realize now I have to go back home. My studies. My mother. I go to a street corner. It looks like St-Denis and de Maisonneuve Boulevard. There are plenty of pedestrians walking hurriedly past. I approach one and ask him how to get home. He doesn't even see me, as though I am a ghost – or a homeless person. I approach two young girls about twenty-years-old. They are well dressed, and look very bourgeois. They walk right past me. Have I become invisible? Finally, I see my own mother. She is walking with two police officers, a man and a woman. I call out to her, "MOM!! MOM!!" But she stares right at me and doesn't recognize me. Either that, or she doesn't even see me. Oh my God, I want to break down and cry. And time seems to be going by so fast. It seems like I have been in this other dimension for weeks, months. I feel my face with my hand, and my beard has grown. I look down at my clothes, and they are all ripped and shredded. And there are holes in my shoes. Am I here all alone? Where are my friends? Where is Mary Wells? What has happened to me?

Now I am starting to get hungry, and there are no restaurants around. All the stores are boarded up. I see a garbage can, and there is a delicious-looking slice of pizza sitting right on top of the pile of rubbish. Hey, I am not proud, and I am so hungry that I grab the slice of pizza and eat it. Now I feel sick. I ate too fast. And I realize that I have lost weight in the past while. It seems that night and day are all the same.

Now I want to phone my mother, but I have lost my wallet. So I stick my fingers in a pay phone, in the coin return. No, there are no quarters in there.

And I am getting tired. I don't know if it is morning, noon or night. I find an alleyway where I won't get bothered. So I lie down on a piece of cardboard, out of the way of pedestrians. I fall asleep within minutes.

Time goes by. I am sleeping on my piece of cardboard. The snow is falling. Snowflakes from heaven are falling. Falling. I am covered in cardboard. It seems like weeks and weeks have gone by. Finally, a stray dog licks my face, and I wake up. My bones are sore. My back and legs are sore. I am frostbitten and there is nowhere to go. I yell at people on the street, "Help me, help me!" But no one can hear me. I am in a parallel universe, or so it seems. They can't hear me, and I can see them but they don't even see me.

Finally, I see another dude from the streets. He can see me, or so it seems. He is Chinese, I notice. Or maybe Korean, I can't tell. He speaks to me. He wanders up to me, and smiles at me. I say to him, "Cold." He answers, "Cold." And he smiles.

We wander off together. He is about forty or eighty or a hundred years old. I can't tell. He takes me down an alley, and we find other street people sitting around a campfire. They are burning cardboard boxes, shards of wood, planks and toasting their hands by the fire. It is a little fire. It feels good. No one speaks my language. But I sit down at my place by the fire. And it feels good. One man next to me smiles at me. And it feels good.

The night comes down and it is snowing a gentle snow. A few flakes land in the fire and crackle. It feels good. It is warm and there is light.

LIFE AFTER DEATH

The past few years have been a long, strenuous struggle; you went further and further downhill, getting drunk, living on the streets, eating out of garbage cans and at soup kitchens, hanging around drop-in centers, sleeping in women's shelters, occasionally finding enough money for a room at the YWCA, and eventually returning to the streets, sitting in McDonald's at 3:00 o'clock in the morning, drinking, using needles, until finally you are a walking, talking disease, and you end up in the Emergency of some godforsaken hospital, with hepatitis C and AIDS and God knows what else. You felt like you could just lie down and die.

But one evening, you walk into this place. There is a door, back there, that you just walked through. There is a light there, at the end of the tunnel, and you go through a second door, only to find yourself in a room full of strangers. Someone shakes your hand at the door: what the hell is this? There is a woman dressed in a white gown, shaking your hand, and she asks you, "Are you new?" You don't know what to say. New to what? New in what? What are you doing here? Who are these people?

The woman in the white gown smiles at you and says, "Coffee is ready, right over there. Come right in, you're in the right place." How does she know you are in the right place? Nevertheless, you walk over to the coffee urn, and pour yourself a cup of warm coffee in a styrofoam cup. There is sugar and milk on the table. Someone must have known you were coming and that you needed a coffee.

There are chairs lined up facing a conference table. There are two posters hanging from the rafters of the ceiling, with incomprehensible gibberish printed on them. One says something about "steps" and the other, "traditions." Where the hell are you this time around?

People, men and women, but no children, are milling about, chatting in little clusters of two or three. There is no music playing; the building looks like a church basement, but strangely enough, you can't hear any organ music. It is incredibly quiet, as though everyone had come back from the dead. Everyone seems to be minding their own business, and it is quiet. No one is raising their voice, and people are coming towards you to fill up on coffee. One other lady walks up to you and shakes your hand again. What is this business of shaking hands all the time? Don't they know that is how you catch colds and flu?

She says to you, "Hi, what's your name?" And for a split second, you can't remember. You answer her, "It's funny, but I can't remember."

She giggles and replies, "That's okay, if you are new, it is normal that you have trouble talking. Did you have trouble finding us?"

And you answer: "I don't know, I just ended up here, as though I was led here."

She answers, "And rightly so. Do you drink?"

You blush, and you get defensive: "Why? What's it to you?"

But she is not taken aback; she just says, "That's okay, it is all right. The only requirement for membership is a desire to stop drinking. You see, all the people here, all the people you see are just like you. We have already been through hell. This is just a relief, isn't it?"

And suddenly, you realize that you have died, and this is life after death. Not quite what you expected, no organ music, no harp playing, no wings, just coffee and a meeting of people chatting. Hmm, very strange. You are starting to get accustomed to where you are.

Maybe these people aren't so crazy after all. Maybe, like they say, you are in the right place.

The woman is still there, and she says to you, with light and serenity in her eyes, "Nothing will be expected of you. All the jobs have been done. Just grab a seat and enjoy the meeting. No one will lay a trip on you. No one will ask you for money. Besides, we have no use for money in this place."

So you sit down, hesitantly. Other people are sitting down around you, in rows, on wooden chairs that squeak when you move. You are a bit confused, but this seems well organized, anyway, whatever it is. A man at the conference table bangs his gavel on the table and starts the meeting. He gives his name, and then says loudly: "It is customary to begin this meeting with a moment of silence, followed by the serenity prayer."

There is indeed a moment of long silence, then everyone starts chanting this gibberish that you don't understand. But it only lasts for a second. Then the chairman of the meeting goes on.

"Welcome to Life after Death." And your mind drifts off. And the chairman's voice becomes meaningless chatter, as you start remembering the endless drinks flowing, the syringes, the robberies, the crime, the bankruptcies, moral and financial, and you are not listening anymore to what the chairman is babbling about, and you wonder why you ended up in this place, when you deserved to be in hell. And suddenly, you realize that you have already paid your dues, you have already been through hell on earth.

Yes, maybe that is it. The car accidents, the blackouts, the wife battering, the children screaming because they had no food, and finally, the streets. Yes, the streets. Long walks through the snow, with holes in your boots, trying to get out of the cold and the wind. Walking, always walking, like a zombie. And all those men always hitting on you, trying to get a piece of tail out of you, for what? What was their problem? But you realize that you weren't very nice either, yelling at your husband, you remember how totally selfish you were, especially when someone came between you and your booze. And towards the end, before you passed away, you were always in a rage.

Something snaps you out of your reverie. There is a woman sitting at the conference table, and she just said something that caught your attention: "You need to know rage to qualify to be here!"

Now that is strange, uncanny, weird. You were just thinking about rage. And now, the rage seems to be gone. For now. One day at a time. Just what were you so angry about? Oh yes, being a woman in a man's world! No, what was it? Being a native in a white man's world! No, that was not it either.

Then you spot someone in the row behind you, someone you used to know when you were still alive. Can it be? Yes, it is your cousin, and he has just spotted you. He is waving at you, with one hand, and holding a cup of coffee with the other hand. He is sitting there, dead as a doornail, and yet, moving and smiling at you. You smile back, a funny, shy little smile. And then you look in front at the conference table, and the meeting goes on. People are talking and making presentations. One guy is standing up and offering a silver coin to any newcomers. Is this some kind of scam? You just sit there, waiting for the meeting to end, so you can grab another coffee.

But the meeting goes on, for a century or two, for hundreds and hundreds of years, although it feels like an hour. You are just looking around, trying to get your bearings. And you look at yourself, and you too are wearing a white robe. I guess you have been through the great tribulation they talked about in the Bible, but there are no Bibles in sight.

You try to read the posters with the steps and traditions. You see the word "God" and that seems reassuring. But you don't understand the rest of the words.

And you start asking yourself, "If I am dead, and this is life after death, when will I meet God?" And your mind wanders off, as the meeting goes on, for another millenium. This seems like the right place, but no one is preaching at you, no one is asking you for money, there are no stained-glass windows or organs playing.

I guess this is as good as it gets, you tell yourself. People are listening to the speaker, dead quiet, sometimes shifting on the squeaky wooden chairs. And suddenly, you are thinking, "Hey, I am okay here, this is home. This is where I belong. This is all right after all!"

And the meeting goes on into the night. This is the big meeting up in the sky. And you are in the right place.

THE BOYS I MEAN

I am sitting in an all-night restaurant, on the corner of Mont-Royal and St-Denis, in Montreal; it is around 3:00 in the morning, and I am having a coffee while counting my spare change. My rosary is on the table, at my booth, and I have been off my medication for many moons. A couple comes and sits diagonally across from me, and the man is staring at me. He is Vietnamese, and she could be French Canadian. He is staring and staring — so I turn to him, look him straight in the eye, and say to him, "Bonjour, how are you?"

He replies, "Fuck off."

The normal thing to do would be to move to another seat in the restaurant, to leave the restaurant or to just ignore this fellow. What I do — I am off my medication — is that I go see the manager of the restaurant, at the cash register, and I complain that a customer told me to fuck off. He doesn't pay attention. He simply dismisses my complaint and tells me to leave him alone. So I pay my bill and walk out of the restaurant. I go outside — it is June 1984, and it is not cold. I go outside, and wait for the Vietnamese guy to come out. He sees me in the window of the restaurant, and understands that I want to fight with him. He gestures, meaning, you and me, eh? And then he comes out of the front door.

The first thing he does is that he punches me in the mouth. He comes out of the restaurant swinging. He connects and cuts my lip. There are a few missed punches, we spar, and then I let out a god-awful "kiai" yell, a type of yell I have learned in martial arts, and I hit him with my right fist, with all my might, on his left cheek. There is blood all over his face. And then his girlfriend comes out of the restaurant and breaks up the fight. She is frantic and screaming. She pulls her boyfriend away.

I have a cut lip and a major cut on my right fist, where my little finger is. So I phone for an ambulance, and they come, within ten minutes. The paramedics take me to the Hotel-Dieu hospital. I wait for a few minutes at the Emergency ward, and then they stitch up the cuts, on my face and my hand. It turns out I fractured the little finger on my right hand, when I hit the guy. The doctors put a cast on my right hand and wrist.

Then a policewoman comes in and arrests me. She is wearing her uniform, and she handcuffs me. Apparently, my Vietnamese opponent has charged me with assault.

So by 6:00 o'clock in the morning, I am in a cell at Parthenais Detention Center, in the East end of Montreal. It is a little room, with bars instead of a door, with a metal bunk bed, a writing desk that I guess we eat from, as well as a toilet and a sink. There is also a locker where I can hang my clothes. Some time later, the guards bring us breakfast.

No one is allowed to wear a watch here. So we do time, and soon enough, I understand what the penalty is here: time. There is nothing to do to pass the time. So I say my rosary. Soon, I borrow books from the prison library. I start reading Pascal's report to a provincial superior about the Inquisition, Will Durant's history of philosophy, and some books of Leonard Cohen's poetry. I am cozy in my little cell, and in time, the authorities find out that I am supposed to take medication, so they put me back on my prescription of neuroleptics.

Meanwhile, I am hearing voices: I imagine I can hear God himself speaking to me in my mind. I see things that aren't there, like the sink changing appearance, molding itself into various faces. I get exalted feelings, which I think are mystical experiences, as I pray. Basically, I am delusional. But this makes it easier to endure this situation. There are no women, no children, no plants, and no animals. Everything is made of metal and cement.

I spend a week or two in this institution, waiting for my court appearance. I go to court shipped in the paddy wagon. I remember telling a prison guard that I am praying to get out of here, and show him my rosary. He laughs at me, and tells me that is not what is going to get me out of there. While waiting in a holding cell, I talk to a longhaired guy who is a pimp, and he is very uptight, pacing back and forth in the cell. He is obviously very anxious to get out of here.

The guards are pretty rough, and I don't know whom I am more afraid of: the guards or the inmates. The inmates tell the guards racist jokes, and the guards laugh. One day, during a meal, I ask a prison guard for some salt, and he yells back at me that the Hilton hotel is downtown, not here. The inmates call the guards "the screws." Most of the inmates are French Canadians; there are a few blacks, but they are English-speaking; then there are a few more Anglos. There are no other minorities.

The guy in the cell next to mine is a fortuneteller, so the inmates ridicule him by calling him, "Boule de crystal (crystal ball.)" One night, while we are in our cells, I think they are picking on me, because the biggest guy in the ward is yelling at Boule de crystal, and taunting him. I think I am Boule de crystal, so I yell back at Mario, who is also the President of the Sector. I tell him I am not afraid of him, because I have friends in the mafia and friends in the FLQ, a terrorist group. The other inmates start asking each other, talking from one cell to the next, "What is wrong with the new guy?" Another inmate answers, "He thinks he is Boule de crystal." So the next day, one of the inmates tells me I have earned the respect of the others, because they could see "what I am made of." I stood up to the President.

Parthenais Detention Center at that time was a maximum-security prison where people were held pending trial. So there were all kinds of people in there: one guy who was a Raelian had stolen a Beethoven cassette (he was sentenced to two years), whereas other people were in there for murder. Most of them were drug addicts. One day, one of the inmates nicknamed "Animal" describes how his wife has been raped by some fellow; so he shot him full of dimes. Apparently, when you shoot someone with a bullet full of ten-cent pieces, it aggravates the pain. Well, he shot this guy in the balls with a shotgun. And now he is sentenced to ten years in the pen. Another inmate agrees, "When you do someone, you should do him good." And the others all agree.

Frankly, I am terrified of these guys. I figure I will try to get accepted by them, so in order to get extra peanut butter or extra rolling tobacco, I do drawings for the inmates. I draw their portraits, I design tattoos, which a tattoo artist will recopy once they go to Bordeaux jail. And they nickname me "L'Arabe" because I have a swarthy complexion.

They can't play cards or checkers or chess without arguing. They watch television, and one night, there is a Michael Jackson show called *Thriller* and all the boys are gathered around the TV set. Another popular show is the Robert Charlebois' special for Saint-Jean-Baptiste Day. Either way, there is constant noise in the Sector during recess time. The inmates chatter like naked apes in a zoo. It reminds me of the movie *Planet of the Apes*. Another source of irritation is the noise of the doors opening and closing, by remote control, because the cell doors are made of metal bars, which clang shut.

And I wonder what I am doing there. One day, on Saturday morning, we are in our cells, and one of the inmates begins to weep, loudly. Nobody comments.

The prisoners tell me that their girlfriends are topless dancers. And they explain to me how to pick up strippers: you ask a lady to dance at your table, and you tell her you have some cocaine at home. So she comes to your house, and you seduce her. Most of these guys have children. I ask them why they live a life of crime. They all tell me they don't want to work. The common practice is to bribe the judges, so that is what they do. The inmates hate the system, but they play the capitalist game. I ask them what lawyer to get, and they all recommend Wiseman. He is expensive, but he is the best. His practice is on McGill Street, down by the harbour, in the financial district.

So time is going by. One day, a French-speaking prisoner covered with tattoos takes me aside, and asks me, "The guys find you are nervous. What is wrong?"

I explain to him that I am not used to this type of people. He reminds me that inmates are very sensitive people, and he believes they are the most sensitive of all people. I ask him why he is in here, and he says one day when he was a teenager, his girlfriend died in a car crash; ever since, he has adopted a life of crime. He tells me that he is blocked spiritually, and he can't pray.

Finally, a new guy is placed in the cell next to mine, and he tells me that he is the son of a famous wrestler.

He shows me that his front teeth have been knocked out by his father. He tells me that his dad used to beat him up until he was unconscious. So he is in a rage. A couple of days later, things start to turn around.

The son of the wrestler tells me his aunt died that day, so he wants to kill himself. He is looking for a razor blade to slash his wrists. So I don't hesitate — the next time I see him talking to a guard, I barge in and tell the guard to have this guy put in the psychiatric ward, because he wants to kill himself.

And that is the last we see of him.

That night, the inmate in the cell next to mine asks me, in French, "Hey, L'Arabe, you are so cool with the guys! How come you squealed on Vachon?" And I tell him, speaking through the wall, that I did it to save the guy's life. He wanted to kill himself. The other guy answers me, "Sure, sure. We know all about that."

So my life is now in danger, because the inmates consider me an informer. But the next morning, the authorities let me out on bail. I have a court appearance, and my parents are there, and so is my friend Danny. They are ready to post bail.

That summer, I am out of jail, and I have two more court appearances. During the second court appearance, my accuser is supposed to testify, but he doesn't show up. Therefore, the charges are dropped, and I am a free man.

Meanwhile, I rent an apartment on Fullum Street, and I throw a party one night for all my friends who came to visit me in jail. At least while I was inside for a couple of weeks, they put me back on my medication, and I am back on track. Within a month, I go back to doing translation, for the government. It takes a year for the scars to heal and for me to recover from the ensuing depression.

ARE YOU WILD?

By now it is 1985, and you are 36-years-old – are you wild? Is that what you do, keep a perpetual hard-on all day long? You are living in a two-room basement apartment, after getting out of jail, and you have a social worker called Daniel, who takes you out to the movies, to concerts, for meals. Daniel is French from France, and you don't really respect him, because he said some racist things about blacks. He is a theology student who doesn't know God, who has theories about everything, and he is pretty much of a wimp, as far as you are concerned.

Anyway, one day, he brings his girlfriend, Angela, along with him on one of his visits to your apartment. It is summertime, and sweltering hot. You are showing her your writings, and she tells you she is a fan of Henry Miller's. She is Italian, but speaks English to you; she has blue eyes, and short-cropped dirty blonde hair. (You wouldn't kick her out of bed for eating crackers.) Anyway, she is one way while Daniel is around. They visit for a few hours, and you serve them something to drink.

The next time you hear from Daniel and Angela, they are at the airport, and they are off to Cuba or somewhere, and they phone you to say goodbye. You are flirting with Angela, telling her something about getting a suntan all over. She seems to like you, but it is understood she is Daniel's girl.

A couple of days later, someone knocks at your door. You are in your kitchen, and you go answer the door. It is Angela. You are all flustered, because she is throwing a curve at you. You serve her a coffee, and at one point, you are both standing close to each other in the small kitchen, and she brushes against you. You take the cue, and you wrap your arms around her and kiss her, a long, passionate, wet, French kiss, her tongue in your mouth, licking your tongue and palate, like a giant snake entering a cave. When the kiss subsides, you smile at her and ask, "What about Daniel?" And she replies with a wink, "Daniel is only Daniel."

And the roller coaster ride begins. You are living on the corner of Fullum and Sherbrooke, near the old Parthenais prison, and she lives fifteen miles away, in Montreal North. It turns out she has two daughters, one fifteen and the youngest one about eight, and they don't notice you at all. Lovers come and go. Angela tells you, with an insane laugh, that she has the forty-eight hour syndrome – a new lover every forty-eight hours. You are drinking champagne together. She tells you she is fond of corruption, and she says it with a passion. She is addicted to cocaine, or in the process of getting addicted. She is pretty wild. She works at a dating agency, a legitimate dating agency in the heart of downtown. You go see her at work, and you draw portraits of her and her assistant, who is also Italian.

Angela is pathetic however. She was living in France at one time, when her first husband decided to sail across the Atlantic Ocean. He bought a sailboat, and took off. Well, he disappeared. Angela spent five years looking for him. She went up and down the coast of Africa, and heard rumours and tried to keep track of where he had last been seen. But after five years of absence, he was considered missing and dead. Then she remarried three times and got divorced three times. She collected husbands, and now she has the forty-eight hour syndrome.

So you take twenty-dollar taxi rides to her house in Montreal North, and you spend extravagantly together. One time, you are in an outdoor terrace of a restaurant in Montreal North in the hot sun, and she asks you coyly, "What are you staring at?" And you answer, "I was looking at your breast." So she pulls her right breast out of her dress, out of her bra, and lets it hang out where you can see it, right in the middle of the restaurant. You laugh insanely, she laughs insanely, and this is what kind of person Angela is.

And there are plenty of hot, torrid afternoons, in your warm basement apartment, making love passionately on a sofa bed which falls down one time, and that is funny, and you remember that the sex is so hot and passionate, and the summer is so intense, that her black eye liner and mascara are dripping down her face, in streams of sweat, like a big black spider with its claws rolling down her cheeks. And she asks you, after about three hours of wild balling, "Is that what you do? Do you keep a perpetual hard-on all the time?" And in those days, especially if you smoked a joint, you never go soft, and Angela and you make love until you get sore. And that is the essence of this relationship, and you tell Daniel you are fucking his girlfriend, and he is not too amused, but Angela doesn't care about him. Daniel thought he was doing you a favour by taking you out, because you have a mental illness. But he is definitely out of the picture. You have cut his grass, mister.

And the party with Angela goes on, for about three weeks, and it is fast-paced, and wild, and steamy. One day, however, you go by yourself to see a movie called *Birdie*, which sets you off. It is about a Vietnam veteran who is totally gauche with women, and has never had a girlfriend, and when he ends up in a psych ward, he thinks he is a bird, and perches naked on his bed. And this sets off a neurosis in you. You write a letter to Angela. The letter says very weird things about women. Angela is turned off. She tells you it is over. You try to phone her once or twice, but she won't take the call. The party is over, and she has found someone else to replace you. The forty-eight hour syndrome. You feel sad, and bitter. You hear from a friend of hers that she got married again for the fifth time about a year later. This friend is a jazz singer called Ming Lee, and he is in touch with her. You move to Fredericton, New Brunswick, that summer.

"Do you remember, baby, last September, how you held me tight each and every night, and you'll find somebody new, and baby, we'll say we're through, and you won't matter anymore." Later, that summer, you are in Ottawa, visiting your parents, and you go for a beer with your dad in a crowded downtown bar, and the Buddy Holly song is playing on the PA system, and your dad tells you, in French, "That is the tragedy of life, that relationships don't last."

BODHISATTVA DOG

One spring day, I happened to be in a huge Catholic cathedral in Montreal called Mary Queen of the World, on René-Lévesque Boulevard, attending mass, and had trouble concentrating on the mumbo-jumbo of the priest's invocations and liturgy. I looked up at the Latin inscriptions going around the ceiling in four foot high letters that read, "Damnatus est." This was too much, it was the last straw.

So I got out of my pew and began to walk out of the building. It was a long timeless walk but the doors leading to the street were wide open. As I approached the portico, I saw an old lady trying to chase a dog out of the church. Her hands kept beating the air, but the dog insisted – he wanted to get into the building. Until he saw me.

Once the dog and I crossed paths, it turned around and began to follow me out of the cathedral, down the steps to the sidewalk of the busy downtown street in the business area. Or rather, I began to follow the dog. It definitely knew where it was going, and where it was leading me.

This intelligent animal and I had an understanding. He walked at my pace, on the inside of the sidewalk, and I kept up with its lead.

We walked and walked, out of the business area, leaving behind the skyscrapers, down into a poor neighbourhood called Little Burgundy, where there are a lot of black families. The dog had the lead, and took me down St. Antoine Street and St. Jacques Street. It wouldn't slow down. So I figured it knew where it was going.

We came up to a subway station called Georges Vanier metro. Here the doggie stopped and seemed to pause. A mysterious young girl walked up to me. Obviously, here was my destination. She must have been nine or ten. She was wearing a beige dress down to her knees and seemed to come from that area. We began talking, in French, which was now the official language in this brave new world, and I asked her if there were a lot of suicides in this metro station. I told her I had seen records that there are five hundred suicides a year in the Montreal subways. You know, you are riding on the metro and suddenly, it stops. A loudspeaker tells everyone there is an incident and to be patient. Well, these are suicides, and I wondered if there were a lot of suicides at the Georges Vanier metro station. The little girl answered me, "No, not many suicides. Just murders."

This seemed like a revelation, out of the mouth of a seemingly innocent little girl. Meanwhile, the dog had disappeared and I thought of being a saviour in this time and place, but chose instead to go home. There had been many salvations in this province of Canada, but it always seemed necessary to control people and stifle the truth. This child candidly knew the score — so who was I to influence her in any way?

NO SINGULARITIES

The universe had ceased to expand, having reached its outer limit, and had begun to contract. Just like a person from the Northern hemisphere crossing into the Southern hemisphere past the Equator, we were all headed in reverse time towards a South pole without singularities which would consist in an implosion, perhaps as momentous as the big bang.

I for one went from dying in the Emergency of a hospital, with tubes attached to my arms and hooked up to a heart monitor, which beeped alarmingly for all the nurses in the ward, to being an old millionaire gigolo. My girlfriend had inherited her father's fortune in the golf business, and we rapidly spun backwards in time to the days when we were raising babies and changing diapers. Lots and lots of diapers.

In those days, around 1994, I believe, we went on a lot of family outings to the park, because we couldn't afford to travel elsewhere.

Moving back, I remember the first night I met Bonnie, and she came into the room with Dwane Read, and the first thought that went through my mind was. Who's the pretty girl with Dwane? I'm going to cut his grass.

Prior to that, as I regress towards birth, I am sitting on my balcony, while working for the Ministry of Education, and single, and wondering what will happen next in my life — never expecting to have raised kids and moved out of Montreal. I live in a high-rise in 1989, among the roofs of other high-rises downtown, and I am dreadfully lonely.

I rush back to a million bars and night clubs and strip joints, a lonely bachelor high on alcohol and desperation, hanging around with street people whom I am bankrolling, going to mass, writing religious poetry.

And I move back to college days, when I always have my hand up in class, and I'm hanging around with smart alecks from the middle class, and I am spending seven hours a night in reverse at the library, reading Martin Luther and Immanuel Kant, looking up the *Chants du Maldoror* in the stacks in my reverse spare time.

Then I am in seminary school, thirteen-years-old, waiting to be born again, which I am in 1948. In those days, there is no television; the bread man comes by in a horse-drawn wagon, from door to door; there are no supermarkets, and in Ottawa, you still see tanks grinding down the streets in a preview of World War II. My parents are listening to Pius XII on the radio and reciting the rosary after supper along with the radio.

And time is moving backwards, headed towards the big implosion.

It takes my mother fifty-six hours of reverse labour to give birth to me, three weeks late. Then her father dies on the day I am supposed to be born. And later on, he is a young man, working for the government in the Gold Rush in the Yukon, which is far, far away and back in time.

I then remember the Inquisition, the crucifixion of Christ, the early cavemen, in that order, the dinosaurs a hundred million years from now. Because by now I am in eternity, looking at a brief history of time.

And then nothing but stardust spinning around.

Poof.

THEN SUDDENLY WAR ENDED

Nobody really knew why nor how, but this is what happened. There was no election or change of the guard. There was no revolutionary leader influencing others to lay down their weapons. But here and there across the world, like an epidemic, like lightning shining from East to West, one government after another decided to pull their troops out of the war. And within a few weeks, the business pages of local newspapers announced that one arms maker after another, one arms trader after another was converting its armaments factories to peaceful purposes. Was it because the world was tired of fighting? Were the armies out of breath? Not really. But on the front pages of newspapers and in the evening news on TV, people could see one general after another resigning and taking retirement. The good news was that finally, the nuclear powers were showing the will to dismantle their bombs. Had all the world leaders gone mad? What about the enemy? What about the economy, which had relied so much on manufacturing weapons? And yet, the presidents and prime ministers were calmly announcing a new policy worldwide. At some level, it didn't make sense. And those who should be in favour of world peace were the most upset about the new policy of abolishing war. The radicals who used to demonstrate against war now had to find another cause. But the populations of the world just expressed a big sigh of relief. A truce! Finally, a truce! So many thousands of people who used to work in the arms industry had to find new jobs in the new peaceful sector. And yet governments were laying off all the folks who used to manufacture guns and tanks. The new economics books no longer discussed a guns and butter economy. It was now entirely a butter economy. And yet the stock market didn't crash, there were no food riots. It was as though peace spread from one household to another, from one human heart to another. There was no more need for intelligence agencies or spying. There was a new atmosphere of trust in the air. And gradually people began to dance and sing on the streets, in Jerusalem, in New York, in Madrid and Melbourne; suddenly, the oppression of war was replaced with overall joy. People who had invested in the arms business seemed relieved and went on vacation. Instead of soldiers marching through public places, there were tourists and picnics and festivals. Children began carrying flowers. I don't know, I couldn't explain it or understand why, but benevolence now reigned where malice and cynicism had before. Nevertheless it was business as usual – people stopped taking drugs and pushers flushed their heroin down the toilets. Had the world gone mad? Yet everything was peaceful, crime rates dwindled, there was no more need for police. People began cleaning up land mines from war zones and many who used to be militant began helping handicapped victims of war. Suddenly, there were funds released for veterans and rehabilitation programs were created for former soldiers. In areas where war was not visible, the news came out that local businessmen used to invest in arms and banks shut down any investment which wasn't green. Parks were built slowly but surely in areas where there had been gunfire. There was gradual reconciliation between conflicting nationalities and religions. This process had begun suddenly, but snowballed until peace reigned in every heart. Little boys stopped playing with toy guns and war videos. In schools, teachers ceased to teach about the enemy out there. People started realizing that Russians and Chinese people were just like us, and the propaganda machine ground to a halt. Happiness started to spread all over the world. Fear and paranoia were now a thing of the past. And love was no longer a dirty word.

THE CONVERT

I first met this guy Smitty in the fall of 1969. He was living at his friend's place in NDG, Montreal. I was working as a secretary, and after work I would drop in at their apartment, and usually, he would ask me to play a game of chess with him. I found him cute with long dark hair that flowed on his shoulders, and after a few chess moves, he would look at me, point at the bedroom next door, and we would go into the next room, where we would undress and make love for what seeemed like hours. I would smile at him as we made love, with the moon shining on one side of his face, the other side remaining dark and hidden. He would wink at me.

After a whole evening without conversation and lots and lots of seawaves of romance, he would walk me home in Westhaven Village, where I lived alone, kissing several times on the way there, until he would leave me at the doorstep under the moon. It was almost exclusively a physical relationship, except we both had unavowed feelings for each other, and although he had trust issues, we got along well on those terms.

There was a lot of drug use and abuse at his friend's apartment all through that fall, and his brother was a pusher who kept us all supplied with whatever we pleased. There was a coffee shop downstairs, which was a hangout for a lot of younger people. I knew Smitty had been involved in some kind of political scene that fall in Saint Henri, but since we never talked, it was never mentioned.

Suddenly, however, our relationship was interrupted. I went to his friend's place one afternoon after work, and heard Smitty had ended up in the Douglas, in Verdun. What had happened? Most people didn't know. I asked around. I stopped asking questions. I went on with my life, working, dropping by his friend's place and seeing my own friends.

I wasn't very much involved in their drug scene. I smoked the odd joint and never got into trouble. Smitty was twenty-one, I believe, and had been doing a lot of LSD25 with the wrong people.

I didn't hear from Smitty until three months later, in March 1970. I was still working and he came over to my place one afternoon. It was a Saturday. He showed up at my front door, and I asked him, like Mae West, 'Is that a pistol in your pocket or do you really like me?' I thought that would make him loosen up, because he looked very uptight. They obviously had cut off his hair in the funny farm. He couldn't smile anymore. His knees were twitching, his feet were dancing, his fingers were playing an invisible piano. His whole demeanour was a circus.

I thought I would make him relax. We lay down on my sofa and I tried to kiss him. It was like kissing a corpse. He was totally rigid. They had destroyed his personality.

I told him I didn't love him anymore and to please leave. I didn't want any trouble.

I went on with my life. I got laid off my job as a sec-retary, so I went back to university and became a nurse. This took a few years. In 1973 or 1974, I don't remem-ber the exact date – I remember bumping into Smitty in the elevator at the Queen Elizabeth Hospital, where I worked. I was wearing a uniform and there were several people in the elevator with us. He looked even goofier than before. I didn't want him in my life again. I kind of smiled at him and told him I was working as a nurse. He was on heavy medication by now. He drooled, try-ing to smile. This was embarrassing. I didn't want to be seen with this guy. I got off at the third floor, and told him I would talk to him some other time. There was no way I was going to have a relationship with some loser on neuroleptic medication. Those guys are likely to do anything.

Eventually, I got married and settled down. I had two kids. My new husband was great. We stayed together for several years, and then – I bumped into Smitty again. This time, it was on Sainte Catherine Street, near the corner of Bishop. At first, I didn't rec-ognize him. He now had a beard, a big black beard, and short hair with John Lennon glasses. He accosted me as I was walking down the street.

He was no longer all doped up on medication, but he looked stranger than ever. By now he was all doped up on Jesus. He motormouthed at me, telling or rather screaming at me that he had just returned from Berke-ley, California, where he had supposedly seen the light. Wow, bananas! He was working as a street preacher in Montreal. By now, he was no longer trying to get into my pants; he was trying to convert me! What the hell!!? He told me he had been born again and I had to repent and get on my knees and let Jesus into my heart. OK, buddy, like get lost! I listened to his rap for about twenty minutes, waiting for the perfect time to make my getaway. I dismissed his preaching with something like, 'Well, if it works for you, that's great. To each his own…' And I walked away.

The only difference in this last encounter was that he was no longer meek – he had found power. He was practically overwhelming, albeit psychotic. His eyes said it all. The lights were on but there was nobody home.

I went on with my life. I went through a divorce. Got remarried. It's funny what happened to Smitty. Once they got hold of him, he became a guinea pig. They had him on medication, then into cults. I feel sorry for the guy in a way. He seemed at first like just a regular guy. Never saw him again. I wish him well.

PEACE THAT PASSETH ALL UNDERSTANDING

It was one of those lives. My husband was in the hospital, freaking out and bouncing off the walls. He had gone off his medication a few months before, and had gone out of his mind. Mad as a hatter. Mad as birds.

The kids were young and it probably affected them for life. One day, Nathalie, the younger daughter, said to me, as we were walking down the street, "Daddy's not nice anymore. Now there is only you that's nice." He would take the kids in the car, driving erratically, driving up one way streets the wrong way, and screaming, "That goddamn wife! That goddamn wife!" So I would hide the car keys from him behind the washing machine in the basement. He would scream that someone kept breaking into our house and stealing his car keys. He would stay up at night, playing bizarre videos and records that kept the kids awake. He had lost all sense of affection and slapped the kids. One time, Nathalie cut herself because she had been jumping up and down on the bed, an accident happened and she had to go to the hospital for stitches and he refused to visit her in the children's hospital, no doubt because he didn't want to get hospitalized, claiming it was "a science fiction hospital." He would walk out of the house, leaving the front door wide open. And he went into rants about his late father, who had also been mentally ill.

73

For hours on end, he would demonize him and accuse him of having been an undercover nazi or of having worked for the police.

Not knowing what else to do, even though he was not a drinker, I went to a meeting of Al Anon one evening, and that was helpful. However, there wasn't much humour or levity in the air. This was a roomful of victims. They discussed how they didn't get involved in their husbands' madness or projections. They had to ward off the blows of their alcoholic partners. I didn't have much of a support group otherwise. There was Angela and there was Beatrice. There was Susan and Karen. But none of them had offspring. They didn't understand what I was going through with my husband. My husband also projected on me, falsely accusing me of listening in on his phone calls. He threatened to get physically abusive and screamed a lot around the house.

This scared the kids, and I knew I had to get him committed. I went to the clinic and made an appointment with his nurse, behind his back. She understood, as this had happened previously. He had developed mental illness when he was a young adult and had been seen at the same clinic for over twenty years. He was almost perfect as long as he took his neuroleptic meds, but when he thought he was cured and didn't take his pills anymore, he would gradually get sick. I told the nurse what he was doing, and she was familiar with his pattern. She took care of everything. We met at the courthouse one cool November morning, as agreed, and I testified before an old judge that my husband needed to be hospitalized. I was very, very nervous. But the judge seemed to be a compassionate man and issued a court order, which is the only way to get a relative hospitalized in this country, and I was told what to do. I had to wait for a time when my husband would be home, and call an ambulance. Then I had to show the paramedics the court order, and they would take him to a psychiatric hospital by ambulance. It all went smoothly, although my husband was furious with me and kept a grudge for a long time that I had curtailed his freedom. I had no choice. He was a threat to the kids.

This was wearing me down and I developed insomnia, just because of my anxiety level, living with a time bomb. Once he was hospitalized, it meant I became a single mom for as long as he was locked up. I hadn't worked in a couple of years and knew I had to go back to work. I was going to be the sole breadwinner for a while.

But first, a miracle happened – well, pretty good synchronicity. A couple of days after he got committed, I was relieved that the nightmare was over – he was temporarily out of the picture. Now, I went to the grocery store to buy some milk for the kids. And suddenly, I realized I had no cash in my bank account and no credit on my VISA card. What was I going to do!!? I came home and thought about it for about five minutes. The kids were at school. None of my friends had any money. All of a sudden, the phone rang. It was a lady from city hall. I wasn't expecting any calls. She said, in French, "Hello, my name is Lise Leclerc. I am calling from Montreal City Hall. Is this Kathy McGuire?" I said I was. And yes, I was a translator. I had worked in that field for twenty years, except for the past couple of years. She went on. "Your husband's cousin gave us your name. We have a temporary job for you, replacing a translator on sick leave. Would you like to start work on Monday?" I said I would. She said there was a formality. Would I go in the next day and take a translation exam from French to English? Yes, I would. It was all set. The next day, I wrote and passed the exam with flying colours. This was on a Friday. The following Monday, I started working. It was too good to be true!

At first, this was tricky. I was alone with the kids. My two daughters were eight and six, and in no way autonomous. I was stuck with the proverbial double burden of home and work.

I woke up early, and had to get the kids up by 5:00 a.m. to get them ready for pre-school. Sometimes they didn't feel like waking up so early, and I had to insist. I had to run a tight ship. In a way, it was simple: there was one single chain of command. My husband wasn't around, sabotaging my plans with his illness. I just couldn't think about him at this point. I had to temporarily shut him out to survive and take care of the kids. Luckily, my daughters were obedient. They knew something was wrong, because daddy wasn't there, but their insecurity made them cling to me and depend on me. I generally didn' t have to repeat myself. The children knew I meant business.

On the other hand, I had no time for other people. My attitude was, "If you can help me, stick around. If you are going to be a nuisance, get lost." When I went shopping with my daughters, I expected old ladies to hold the door for us! I had to cut out all social amenities. I had to push to get through the day. One time, I was short thirty-five dollars to buy a pair of shoes for my other daughter, Madeleine, and I walked into my accountant's office and told him bluntly to give me the money. He was not one to be charitable, but he knew I was desperate. I was serious. He reached into his pocket and gave me the cash.

I had one speed. It was "go." Sometimes, it was "faster." I couldn't let the kids mess around. If we had to leave for school at 7:15 a.m., I couldn't let them slow us down. They had to have their boots on and their hats and coats on by 7:15 a.m. There was zero tolerance for fighting or fussing.

I would make the kids' breakfast, made sure they brushed their teeth and combed their hair. Then their clothes and school uniforms had to be ready, ironed and washed. Their homework had to be done. And then we would walk half a mile to their school. I dropped them off at pre-school, which started at 7:30 a.m. Then I walked one block over, took the bus to the metro station, and sat on the metro for half an hour, so I would arrive at work at city hall on time by 8:30 a.m.

Every minute counted, every second was calculated. However, there were some pleasant fun times thrown into the week. Sometimes, at night, after all their homework was done, we would have activities to entertain them. For instance, we would cut up words out of the newspaper and put them into a hat; then we would in turn pick out words and make up poems and glue the words to a piece of paper. And every evening, I would read them a story from a book before they fell asleep. There were several libraries nearby, and on Saturday afternoons, after the grocery order was done, we would go to the library together. We would borrow amazing kids' books for bedtime reading. I was hoping they would develop a taste for literature later on in life. At one point, I had to cancel the cable TV subscription, because they had stopped reading and were watching too much television. Instead, I bought them all the Harry Potter books, and they read them all. This got them interested in reading. When I read them bedtime stories, Nathalie, the youngest one, would often disrupt and start laughing and fooling around. It was a struggle to be patient.

Every now and then, they would be invited to a friend's birthday party. This meant buying an appropriate present and getting them there on time. It also might mean socializing with other mothers and comparing notes on raising kids. I could also discuss childrearing with my colleagues at city hall. Many of the secretaries and clerical workers there were single moms also. There was an amazing degree of solidarity among us. Once in a while, we would have a coffee break together or eat lunch in a group at the restaurant. It wasn't all desperate being a single mom. However, what I didn't agree with at city hall was the racism against a Haitian woman who worked with us. The other employees felt the food she brought in for her lunch smelled spicy and they would gossip behind her back. And I felt some of the other employees discriminated against me because I had an English-sounding name.

Every penny counted, and I couldn't afford babysitters very often. I rarely used the car and took public transportation as often as possible. Gas is expensive. We didn't eat expensive cheese or cakes. We were still eating meat back then, so that added to the grocery bill. I didn't drink, so there was no alcohol to pay for in the bill. One thing that cost me was doing the laundry, because we didn't own our own washer or dryer. We lived in a high-rise and had to use the machines in the basement. It cost to wash as well as to dry the clothes. Plus it meant taking several trips in the elevator.

I tried to train the children to clean up after themselves, but I don't think I did a very good job of it. They would rarely help with the dishes either. You can't raise perfect kids.

Once a week, on Sundays, we would go visit my husband at the psych ward for an hour. For the longest time, he wasn't getting any better. But I felt it was important that the children see their father, so they would learn compassion and visiting people who are sick. Also they had bonded with him and I wanted them to stay close to him. It wasn't always easy. Sometimes, he would just be angry with me because I got a court order and got him committed. Other times, he would respond to the kids' attention.

I took naps whenever I could. I would get very tired from being on the go all the time. I had no problem falling asleep at night now that I was a single mom, thank god. There was no more stress caused by my husband's antics. I burned up my energy every day and it didn' t take long to fall asleep. The kids also slept well, although Nathalie sometimes wet her bed, and that meant changing the sheets in the middle of the night. I bought them native dream catchers and hung them over their beds, so they fell asleep easily. This reassured them.

This routine went on for about six months, into the following summer. Everything went smoothly. However one morning I was especially tired and got on the subway as usual, went two stops and suddenly, I spaced out. I asked myself why I was doing this, and got off the metro. As soon as I stepped out on the platform, I realized this was a mistake and waited for the next subway to come. But for a split second, I just snapped. I couldn't take the pressure anymore. That day, I was a bit late for work.

I had never realized how much was involved in raising kids, until I had to do everything myself. For example, they regularly grew out of their clothes. It was a lucky thing I could give Nathalie her older sister's hand-me-down clothes, but still it was expensive. Oftentimes, there was no extra money left over. They each had their own bed, which my husband had bought. They didn't have any bicycles. That year, they had adequate winter clothes and skates. On weekends, they sometimes went skating at the community arena. There weren't many accidents. One time Nathalie cut her face while jumping on the bed, but that was before their father was hospitalized. They did catch strepthroat and that involved taking a few days off from school and going to the clinic, but using antibiotics, they recovered promptly. My boss also gave me time off to mind the kids at home.

My older sister, who lives in Ottawa, came for a visit one day and brought the kids presents. I am pretty close to her but she was very busy with her career at that time. Her children were grown up and living on their own. She had a boyfriend called Michel who made the kids laugh with his constant jokes. She came here on a Saturday and Michel did the driving. They stayed a whole afternoon and my sister told me that if I needed anything, to let her know. She was very fond of my kids and I knew she was a responsible woman.

The kids' marks were good in school, although Nathalie's teacher commented that my daughter disrupted the class by chatting with her neighbour. Madeleine was supposedly a quiet child who never said a word in class. Her teachers loved her because she was a serious student and kept her notebooks tidy.

I would finish work at 4:30 p.m., take the metro and a bus to the kids' school and pick them up at 5:30 at after-school. The workers made sure the kids did their homework during this session, which facilitated things for me. We would walk home and have supper. I found however the school nickel-and-dimed us for pizza lunch, and other programs that came up regularly. And I had to pay for the daycare services before and after classes.

By summertime, there were a couple of events at school, like graduation, the end-of-the-year concert and a party in the schoolyard that I had to attend. But now it was time for summer camp. I had saved up to pay for them to attend camp for six weeks. Plus their grandmother bought them clothes and new sleeping bags for camp. After a week of preparations, I drove them to the mall, where all the kids' parents waited for the school buses to arrive. As usual, the buses were late. My kids had proper suitcases and sleeping bags and were thrilled to get aboard the bus. They were supposed to come back home every two weeks and stay in the country in Rawdon for most of the summer. At that time, in 2001, it cost me fifteen hundred dollars to ship them off to camp. And their grandmother chipped in about three hundred for the clothing and sleeping bags. The camp was called Trail's End Camp. It was your low-budget all-purpose summer camp.

In June that year, the employee I had been replacing came back to work from her sick leave. She had had a colon operation which consisted in shortening her intestine. I was notified my term was over.

Right away, I started looking for federal government contracts and landed a short-term job, working out of my office at home.

My husband was recovering, according to the doctors at the psych ward.

My situation was developing. Now one Saturday morning, I had been busy with the translation contract, when I felt chest pains. I had difficulty breathing. My chest felt tight. This lasted from about 10:30 a.m. in the morning until noon. By twelve o'clock, my lungs felt like they were on fire. I was also getting increasingly anxious. At 12:15, I finally called for an ambulance. It arrived within thirteen minutes, with the sirens blaring.

The paramedics came into my apartment on the sixth floor wearing their purple and gray uniforms. They were big husky guys. There was something military about their appearance, but I trusted them. They took my blood pressure and pulse. Then they took my temperature. I told them my lungs were burning. They asked me if I felt pain in my shoulders and arms. I said no. Had I thrown up? No. Had I been drinking? No. I asked them if I was having a heart attack and they replied that maybe so, but only a blood test at the hospital would determine that, because when you are having a heart attack, there is a certain enzyme present in your blood. I told them I was willing to go to the emergency ward. They were very professional about it. They brought in a yellow stretcher and lay me down on it. They tied my hands on my chest with straps and put a blanket over me. Afterwards, they gave me some aspirin to swallow and made me breathe oxygen through a tube that they inserted into my nose. Finally, they gave me a couple of puffs of nitroglycerin, which I took under my tongue. I was in a panic, because I was in a lot of pain, and everything had become extremely intense. But I trusted the paramedics. They knew what they were doing. And they took me to the Verdun Hospital.

***

I remember seeing a pile of dung and a flurry of flies buzzing furiously and feverishly all around it. I remember seeing a whirlwind of dead coloured leaves spinning around, blown by the wild autumn wind. I remember being in the middle of a riot and wondering what I was doing there, as people were running to and fro, as the police charged through the crowd on their motorcycles.

Once we got to the hospital, I got rushed through triage and ushered on a stretcher into the emergency ward, where there were constantly over six nurses puncturing holes in my arms, making me snort nitroglycerin, giving me aspirin to chew, while oxygen kept flowing into my nose through a plastic tube.

Finally, I saw a cardiologist, a man called Dr Maranda, who was over six foot five, and he told me I had had an *infarctus*. The pain gradually subsided, as well as the level of intensity. I was eventually left alone, with tubes coming out of my arms and nose, hooked up to a monitor that recorded my pulse and blood pressure. After a while, the nurses came to see me occasionally to take my blood pressure and make sure everything was all right. These women were very supportive, although they were under a lot of pressure at work. I wasn't the only patient there, and whenever I spoke to a doctor or a nurse, kindness was practised.

I started looking around at my surroundings. There was a curtain that they could wrap around my bed, going around a track on the ceiling. There was an old man in the bed next to mine, judging by his voice, although I couldn't see him. On the other side, there was a teenager covered in tattoos, sleeping with tubes coming out of him. Both patients were white. There were about thirty or forty other patients in the ward, but I couldn't see them. The nurses, orderlies, doctors, cleaners and other staff kept parading past my bed, in and out of the glassed-in nursing station. Behind the glass, I could see but couldn't hear the staff sitting down and talking on the phone, reading charts, going about their business.

You couldn't sleep. There was always someone waking you up.

After a couple of days, I was in the intensive care unit, in a room by myself. This was a big relief. I still had slight pain in my chest. I was provided with a phone and called a couple of people. My sister sent me a bouquet of flowers, which the staff kindly placed in a vase. There was a note from her saying that she would come to Montreal and take care of my kids for me. I was so grateful, because that was a big worry. For the time being, Madeleine and Nathalie were at summer camp. But then what? My older sister took the kids to Ottawa with her eventually, long enough for me to recover from this heart attack.

I met with an older male cardiologist called Dr Malo, who told me I had been lucky to survive this heart attack. He said one of my major arteries was blocked and I would need an angioplasty. He kindly explained the procedure to me: the doctor in the operating room at Notre-Dame Hospital would go in through my wrist, where he would make a small incision, and drive a wire up to my chest and place a crutch called a "stent" into the blocked artery to open it up for circulation. This was going to take place on a Friday that week.

He also told me I had to change my diet. It was a great thing I didn't smoke or drink, because otherwise I would be dead at this point. But I had to stop eating sweets like I did as well as red meat. I would eventually be referred to a nutritionist.

Meanwhile, my arms were all black and blue from all the needles I got. I was hooked up to a monitor and had liquid poured into me intravenously. I told the staff I didn't want visitors. Besides it would just upset my friends to see me in this shape. I slept a lot that week. I wasn't very strong. I remember craving coffee. They fed me bland hospital food and decaffeinated coffee.

I prayed a lot that week. The hospital chaplain came to see me, but I could see right through him. He looked like he was wearing the mask of a joker. He had a perpetual false smile on his face, while his eyes were deep holes of darkness.

I also struggled psychologically against death. I felt Mr Death was standing a foot away from me, waiting to take me. I asked the nurses for some paper and a pencil and did a cartoon of a skull wearing Mickey Mouse ears, and the caption was Mickey Death. It was my way of laughing at the devil. Still, he was standing right by my bedside waiting for me to go.

My friend Angela mailed me a card wishing me speedy recovery. Others phoned. I was relieved that I didn't have to deal with a barrage of visitors to entertain.

I just wanted to relax and prepare for the angioplasty. Finally, Friday came around and that morning, a Haitian nurse came to take me to the Notre-Dame Hospital. They wheeled my bed out of the intensive care unit and down endless halls, as I stared at ceilings and more ceilings. Then we took a taxi together to the other hospital, which is on the East side of Montreal, across the street from Parc Lafontaine. Once we arrived at the hospital, I was laid down on a stretcher again, and we waited and waited for my turn in the operating room. The nurse didn't say much to me, but she did comment that most women who had the same type of heart attack as I had didn't survive.

I realized I wasn't very strong. My turn to be operated came around noon. The doctor who operated on me told me, when I asked him, that had I been smoking or drinking at the time of my operation, I would emphatically be dead now.

There was a camera above the operating table, where I could see what they were doing inside of me. An attendant had shaved me the night before, and the doctor sent the tube in through my wrist. It didn't hurt, but it felt weird, like you would imagine shooting drugs or anal sex would feel like. The tube going through my veins felt cold, and I could feel the snake slithering through my body. Finally, the crutch was installed and after half an hour or so, it was over. I was wide awake through the whole operation. I was glad when it was over, because I had been told there was one chance out of a thousand of either paralysing during the operation, having a second heart attack or dying on the table.

I was taken to a recovery room with my nurse, where I waited until around eight o'clock at night, for an ambulance to take me back to the Verdun Hospital. I remember I was so weak that at one point, she had me get out of bed and try to walk. This was extremely difficult, as I felt my body weighed nine hundred pounds. I had absolutely no strength in my legs to carry me. I walked about two or three feet away from the stretcher and almost collapsed. The nurse didn't say much, but she watched me constantly.

After supper (I wasn't given any food), they wheeled my gurney down the halls again to the ambulance, which was waiting for me.

The next morning, at the Verdun Hospital, I woke up in the intensive care unit again and was given final instructions before my discharge. There were lots of heart pills to take, follow-up appointments to make, as well as instructions on healthier living. It was suggested I exercise more, if I could, and avoid eating steak or creamy soups. I was supposed to show up to meet with a whole troop of cardiologists in the following weeks. It was confirmed that my sister would be taking care of my children for the next while. Also, since I might be weak at first, I was provided with a "meals-on-wheels" service that would come to my house and bring me food every day. At my request, the government had been notified that I couldn't finish the translation contract I had started and couldn't work for several months.

I was finally given a taxi ticket to go home, with a clean bill of health.

***

I had been back at home for a couple of days, when I began to look around my surroundings and get my bearings. When I first came home, I slept for two or three days and ate what they brought me through "meals-on-wheels." I still felt very weak after the angioplasty.

It started to dawn on me that I had had a heart attack and therefore had a close brush with death. This didn't scare me somehow. Maybe I felt afraid deep down inside, but some kind of animal courage to survive kept me going at this point. I would see the sun rise, and this would inspire and encourage me to carry onwards.

I remembered I had prayed a lot while I was in the hospital. I am not a religious person, but the urgency of the heart attack and subsequent operation led me to call out for help. I didn't know whom I was praying to, but I felt grateful to whoever was out there because I pulled through and survived this crisis. Now I needed strength to merely get through the day. I was forced to slow down.

I looked around at my apartment. At OUR apartment, because the kids' clothes lay all over the place, the beds had not been made when they left for summer camp. I could see their running shoes in their closet, and it was *as t*hough the children were still around. I thought of cleaning up their room, but told myself it could wait. I had to recover before I could start a major house *cleaning*. I phoned my sister and she was preparing to go pick them up for the weekend. They had been at camp for over a week.

I spent a lot of time thinking, and it occurred to me maybe I should go to church to thank God I was still alive. OK, there was a Catholic church less than a block away, just up the street. So I walked up to the building with the pointy steeple, painfully, dragging my feet.

There was a service going on when I got there. I sat down in the back row and watched. I sat there for an hour or two, thinking things over. I wondered how come all the major figures in this religion, according to the stained glass windows, were men. God the father was a man, Jesus was a man, all the apostles were male, the pope and the cardinals and the priests were men. Where was there room for women in the Church? There was the Virgin Mary, but the statues of her didn't look very vibrant. Besides, she was some kind of female eunuch. My mind was drifting in and out of a reverie, and these thoughts were going through my mind. Also, all the books of the Bible had been written by men.

Sitting at the front of the church, there were a dozen old ladies, over seventy years old. They all had white hair in perms. And the priest was mumbling something I couldn't hear. As I said, I was near the back door that led to the street.

Still, I felt grateful that Something, Someone out there had helped me survive my heart attack. I wanted to learn more about this power. I gradually gathered my things and put them into my purse, and got up, and walked out of the building. I was relieved to get away from the people inside. I could just picture them burning a witch at the stake or something. That seemed a bit drastic, but I knew enough history to realize those things had happened. I had been raised Catholic, and hadn't given it much thought since I was an adult. Nevertheless, something told me not to talk to the people inside the building. I felt like an outsider. And yet, I knew the Presence that dwelt inside that edifice. There was definitely a vibe, a power that gave me peace while I was in there.

I made up my mind I was going to do research on this Power, the force that kept me alive. Mind you, the next thought was: when is going to be my next heart attack? Will the next one be fatal? This thought gave me a tight chest. I still had plenty of anxiety. And I needed to find peace.

I had arrived back home. I made myself a sandwich, out of the leftovers in the fridge. I didn't feel like cooking very much. As a matter of fact, I didn't feel very motivated to do anything. My little walk to the church had drained me physically, although I felt inspired to research spirituality. I decided to take a nap.

I had a dreamless sleep and when I woke up, the sun was shining on me through the window facing west. I blinked and blinked again. At least the sun wasn't hard to figure out. It was always there. I felt energy once again. The sleep had given me strength.

It seemed like just a couple of weeks before, I had been rushing off to work at city hall. I missed the kids. I thought about my husband. Was I going to take him back? That was a big question. It sure was a chore raising kids by myself. But he was sick in the head, I thought. Was it safe? I postponed thinking about this. I would go for counselling on this issue.

I drifted off to sleep again, in and out of a fantasy. And that is how the days went on, for a few weeks. I felt thrilled to be out of the hospital, I loved the sunshine and fresh air, I would look at the blue summer sky and see the birds circling around, and it all felt great, but I was so small, and so weak. Basically, I felt glad to be alive, which I hadn't felt in years. I had been on a treadmill for several months. Suddenly, I started thinking there was a meaning in my life. I was receiving some kind of grace, and it seemed urgent to find out about this power that was waking me up spiritually.

★★★

I discovered Emily Carr. One day, a few weeks after I went to church, I decided to go to the library. It was in the afternoon, and great streaks of gray light came shooting through the large windows of the building, as I browsed the stacks, looking mainly at picture books. I found two or three large books containing colourful paintings by Emily Carr, the artist of British Columbia. As soon as I looked at her depictions of the forests out West, with their great swirls of energy rushing from the ground to the sky, colour patterns around the great trees, I had a direct response, a gut reaction, identifying immediately with this woman, at a deep primitive level. I sat down with a couple of these books at a table and read about the serpentine force, a power the Theosophists had felt coming out of the Earth. This was contact with the Goddess, I thought, and perhaps this was a clue to my recovery.

I browsed on the library's computers and borrowed a couple of books by Theosophists, from around 1900. There was a book called *Esoteric Christianity*, by an author I didn't know called Annie Besant. There was another book by a fellow called Ledbeater, about the chakras, but this struck me as flaky. And there was a book by Madame Blavatsky, but I never opened it once I got back home.

I remember the part in the book by Annie Besant where she discussed the "kaw," which is what remains of a person's soul on earth after they die. It can be felt for a few days.

This led me to return to the library a couple of days later and do research on authors like Carl Jung,

Wilhelm Reich and R.D. Laing. I read parts of books by Jung and one whole book by Reich called *The Murder of Christ,* and these spoke to me. I felt Reich was in touch with the psychic energy in the universe. He called it the orgone, I believe. He believed in the genital embrace, as opposed to crude sex. I didn't have the courage to read the entire huge volume entitled *The Mass Psychology of Fascism,* but I glanced at it.

All this reading took up a lot of time and energy. I thought also of going back to work, when I received a translation contract from an agency in Toronto. It had been about a month since I had worked, and I honestly believed I could do this work. The job involved a collective agreement between hotel employees and management. I did a few paragraphs, but had to stop. I felt bad for the client, because they really trusted me. However, I felt chest pains and that was a wake-up call to stop working. The people in Toronto were not amused, but the manager of the agency understood. Her secretary thought I was being a wimp. They never gave me work again…

I was flat on my back again until late August, when my kids finished their stay at summer camp. It was arranged with my sister that she would mind them until I was back on my feet. I spoke to them on the phone, and they were worried about me. They wanted to know how their father was. But I told them they could trust my sister to take care of them.

Meanwhile, I had multiple appointments with cardiologists, who prescribed pills and more pills. One doctor had me run on a treadmill, but she determined I did not have angina. Nevertheless, I was given a dispenser of nitroglycerine in case I couldn't breathe and thought I was having a second infarctus. These appointments took a lot of energy and taxed me emotionally and physically.

The amount of walking I did helped a bit, and I was gradually getting stronger. I still had the services of "meals-on-wheels" and the women who delivered the meals were very sweet. But I realized I might have to stay on welfare for the time being. I took my pills religiously. And I reported to the cardiologists every couple of weeks.

Throughout this period, I felt blessed. There is no other word for it. I did feel grateful, and the professionals I dealt with were very kind. I was discovering the big picture, because I thought about things. Sometimes, I would lie awake at night, and invoke the Goddess. Other times, I would pray to Jesus. I also read part of the Upanishads, and discovered the Buddha. His parables spoke to me, and I felt sustained spiritually whenever I opened a book about him.

I hadn't had time to read much during the whole period when I was raising my children, except for their textbooks and the children's literature I read them at night. This was like a vacation. I dreamed I was running, running at full speed, over trees and obstacles like rocks. I was running, and just enjoying the race. I wasn't going anywhere. Just running.

And I kept thinking about the spiritual paintings of Emily Carr, and sometimes I felt swept away by their force. "La force tellurgique," as they called it in French: the serpentine force. I definitely felt carried during these few weeks.

Whenever I thought about single mothers, about divorced women, I had a sense of sisterhood. We definitely had a bond together, which was stronger than oppression or death.

I remembered something my daughter Nathalie had told me one day, when she was in my arms. We had been waiting for her sister one afternoon. Madeleine was supposed to arrive on the little yellow school bus. It was winter and I had pointed out the sunset and purple and gold clouds on the horizon. I told Nathalie, "See? That is what God looks like." She had answered me, with her high, squeaky voice, "Can God sometimes look like a little girl?" I thought about it for a minute and had replied, "Yes, Nathalie, sometimes God can look like a little girl…"

***

Altogether, I spent about two or three months recovering from my heart attack. Meanwhile my kids stayed with my sister in Ottawa. She had registered them in a school near her place and they were doing just fine. I was relieved that they didn't lose a grade because of changing schools. I talked to them almost every day once they came back from summer camp, I missed them, but also appreciated the rest I was getting from the rat race. During this period, I learned that each day was different, and to take it one day at a time. I read a lot, went for short walks and then longer walks, looked at the trees and the flowers and the clouds, talked to my friends and enjoyed my life a bit more every day. I had learned to stop and smell the roses, rather than running constantly, like a hamster in a cage. I found peace of mind.

Meanwhile, I was out and about sometimes during rush hour, when all the people in the neighbourhood were going off to work. One day, I stood on a bridge over an expressway and watched a hundred thousand drivers driving in a hundred thousand cars going off to a hundred thousand meaningless jobs. All for what? For money. You could see the pollution in the air on top of the city: a big dirty, yellow and gray cloud. I wondered if it was all worth it. I knew how these people lived, the empty lives they lived. They came home from work and watched television after supper. It seemed like a big waste of time.

I kept going to the library and the museum and wandering around like a homeless person. I felt peaceful all right, but there was something missing. First of all, my kids were in Ottawa with my sister. But it was more than that. I needed a purpose. We all know about evolution, we know the human race and the entire universe are growing, from century to century, from millenium to millenium. And one evening, I asked myself, Should the entire city, the entire civilization go on strike? Should we stop everything? Should we do like the hippies and live like vegetables and just smoke pot?

I thought about this for a couple of days, for a week or two. And then it occurred to me that no, we carry on. We put our shoulder to the wheel and push – one day at a time, we try to solve the social problems, we make the effort to improve our lot and the lot of our fellow human being. I thought of all the possible situations, and it seemed that mine was not so bad. This meant there was a meaning to all the efforts being made worldwide. The wheels of industry had to keep churning out products and services. The government had to keep charging taxes. The writers and artists had to keep producing works of beauty and meaning and truth.

And we all had to help each other out, each person in their own little way. We were all in this together. We were not islands.

I was determined to recover from my heart attack, and I was going to start living my life again, but wide awake. I was going to remember these few weeks of rest and recovery. I was going to remember what I had learned.

First of all, although pacing myself and listening for any possible chest pains, I started cleaning up our house. Bit by bit, room by room, I tidied up. It took me a few days, at a slow pace. And I found I got stronger by making an effort.

Then I made arrangements to go visit my kids in Ottawa at my sister's house. Within a couple of days, I took the car and drove there. Madeleine and Nathalie were happy to see me. They wanted to know everything I had been doing. They were concerned about their father but I reassured them he was all right. I spent about three days at my sister's house. Finally, it was agreed that they would finish the school year in Ottawa and then I would take them back. I would visit like this on a regular basis. My sister wanted to make sure I got a lot of rest.

As for my husband, I decided not to take him back. I was better off alone than taking care of him. And it was the right decision. He got worse instead of better. Once he got out of the hospital, he went off his medication again. This time he did not recover. I saw him occasionally, first of all in court during the divorce procedures and later on, I met him a couple of times over coffee. He was still bitter that I had gotten him hospitalized, plus he imagined other things. He was full of resentment and I had no time for this.

It was terrible I had lost my husband, because once upon a time we loved each other. But he chose a path I couldn't follow. I felt guilty for dumping him for a few months, but it took him years to recover.

Life went on and I found serenity. I remember going on top of the mountain that is in the middle of Montreal, Mount Royal, and looking at the horizon. I had found faith, faith in a higher power, faith in life, and faith in myself. With this came peace, the peace that passeth all understanding.

ACKNOWLEDGMENTS

I would like to thank a few people without whom this book would not have been possible.

First I am thinking of Dr Todd Swift, who has patiently read all my numerous and sometimes annoying emails over the past dozen years. He is a brilliant and generous soul who has organized this whole publication.

I would also like to extend my thanks to Ann Diamond, who introduced me to Todd and who has given me much support over the years.

Then there is my wife Bonnie McLean, who keeps me on track and has driven me to the hospital many times in the middle of the night. Along with her there are my beautiful daughters Isabelle and Cordelia – I owe them amends for not being a perfect dad.

Also my mom and dad, my sister Claire and my cousin Jean deserve credit for everything here along with the dozens and dozens of teachers and professors and revisors like Yolande Guibord who trained me and taught me everything I know.

Finally I need to mention Brentley Frazer and Ray Fraser and Robert Cheatham and Tod Davies and Glenn Cheriton: these are the publishers who encouraged me and made my writing public.

Thanks once again to people like Julia Schreck and Philip Amsel who were there for me too.

"The author would like to thank the Conseil des arts et des lettres du Québec *for the financial assistance they provided while I wrote certain stories herein."*

CPSIA information can be obtained
at www.ICGtesting.com
Printed in the USA
LVHW040423160121
676611LV00004B/244

9 781913 606268